**LADYBIRD BOOKS, INC**.
**Auburn, Maine 04210 U.S.A.**

**LADYBIRD BOOKS, LTD.**
**Loughborough, Leicestershire, England**

Printed in U.S.A.

Busy Beavers

# MILO the MECHANIC

By Cathy East Dubowski
Illustrated by John Speirs

**Ladybird Books**

Milo Beaver is the best mechanic in town.
His garage is always crowded.
Today is a special day for
Milo. He hopes it won't be
too busy in the garage.

But soon, Mr. and Mrs. Rabbit—and their 27 bunnies—bring in their old green station wagon.

"This old car is as slow as a tortoise," says Mr. Rabbit. "Can you figure out what's wrong?"

"I'll do my best," says Milo.

Milo looks under the hood. He checks the radiator and the engine. "Hmm, it needs some oil," he says.

"We'll pick it up at six o'clock!" says Mrs. Rabbit.

Just then, the phone rings. It's Dr. Bill.
"My car won't start," says Dr. Bill. "I
think my battery is dead! Can you help me?
I'm in a hurry to get to the hospital!"
"I'm on my way," says Milo.

"A jump start should do the trick," says Milo. He hooks up his truck and the car with jumper cables. Then he starts his truck.

*Varoom!* Dr. Bill's car roars to life.

"Thanks, Milo! You're a lifesaver!" says Dr. Bill.

On the way back to the garage, Milo sees a car in trouble.

"I forgot to put on my parking brake!" Mrs. Goat wails. "My car rolled down the hill."

Milo pulls the Goats' car
out of the ditch.
"Yay!" shouts Billy.
"Yipes!" shrieks Eunice.
"We've got a flat tire!"

"Oh, dear!" says Mrs. Goat. "And I've got a million things to do by six o'clock!"

"Don't worry," says Milo. He jacks up the car. "I'll have this spare tire on before you know it."

"Hooray!" shout the kids.

Back at the garage, the bike club needs air—in all 20 tires!

And Milo's friend Rodney Ram needs gas for his lawn mower. "I've got three more lawns to mow by six o'clock," he says.

Milo is very busy now. As soon as he begins one job, someone brings in another thing to fix.

His cousin Burt brings in his pickup truck—
he needs a hinge on
the door repaired.

And his grandmother's gear shift is stuck.

"Can you fix it by six o'clock?" they both ask at once.

The police chief needs a new headlight.
And the librarian's motorcycle has a broken horn.

"I guess you'd like these fixed by six o'clock?" asks Milo.

"That's the ticket!" says the police chief.

"Oh, Milo," says the librarian. "You read my mind!"

Milo works hard all afternoon. He promised *everyone* the work would be done by six o'clock.

Will he finish on time?

One by one, his friends pick up their cars and trucks. At last Milo is ready to go home. "What a busy day!" he thinks. He's tired but happy. He's proud of his good work—and that he's gotten everything done on time.

Milo straightens up his workshop and puts away his tools. But just as he's about to lock up, the phone rings. Somebody needs a mechanic on Woodchuck Way—as soon as possible!

"I'll be right there!" says Milo.

Milo jumps in his tow truck and drives to Woodchuck Way.

But when he gets there, he sees a strange sight: the green station wagon, the lawnmower, the police car, the bikes... *everything* Milo worked on today! Why are they all *here*?

"Oh, no!" thinks Milo. "Didn't I fix them right? Did they break down again?"

"Surprise!" shout all his friends. Milo can't believe it. He's been so busy that he almost forgot what day it is. But his friends didn't forget!

"Happy Birthday," they shout.
"Happy Birthday to the best mechanic
in town!"

Here are some of Milo's favorite tools.

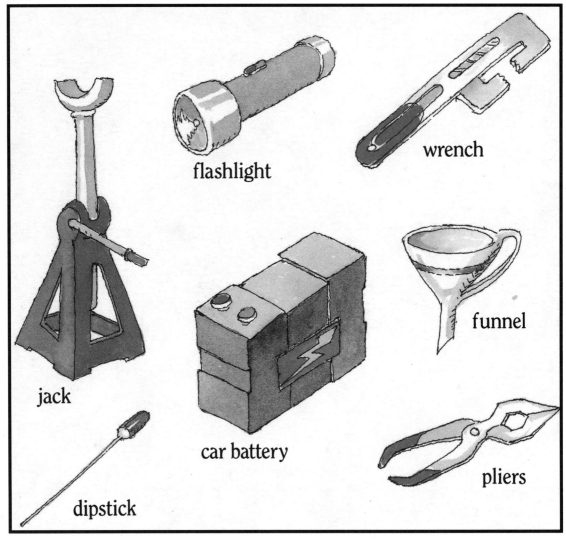

jack

flashlight

wrench

funnel

car battery

dipstick

pliers